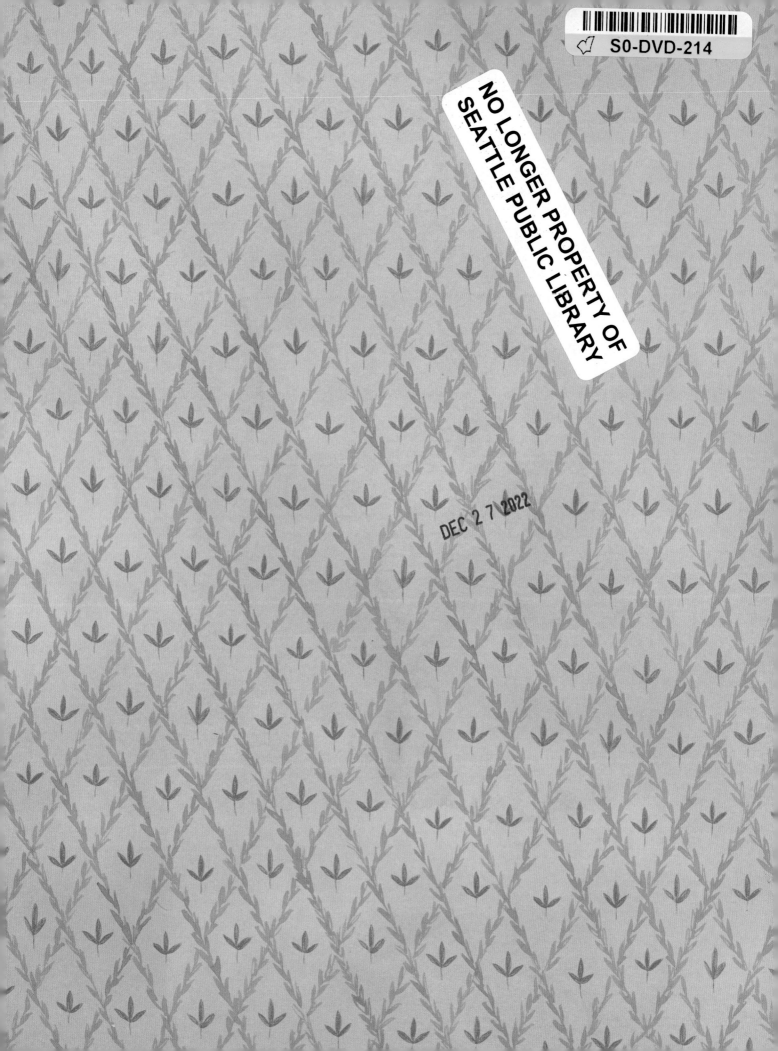

For Tara Walker, with gratitude — L.B.

For my sweetest husband, Martin — I.F.

Tundra Books, an imprint of Tundra Book Group,
a division of Penguin Random House of Canada Limited

LIBRARY AND ARCHIVES CANADA CATALOGUING IN PUBLICATION

Title: Arthur who wrote Sherlock / written by Linda Bailey ; illustrated by Isabelle Follath.
Names: Bailey, Linda, 1948- author. | Follath, Isabelle, illustrator.
Identifiers: Canadiana (print) 20210283084 | Canadiana (ebook) 20210283091 |
ISBN 9780735269255 (hardcover) | ISBN 9780735269262 (EPUB)
Subjects: LCSH: Doyle, Arthur Conan, 1859-1930—Juvenile literature. | LCSH: Holmes, Sherlock—
Juvenile literature. | LCSH: Authors, Scottish—19th century—Biography—Juvenile literature. |
LCSH: Authors, Scottish—20th century—Biography—Juvenile literature. | LCGFT: Biographies.
Classification: LCC PR4623 .B35 2022 | DDC j823/.8—dc23

Published simultaneously in the United States of America by Tundra Books of Northern New York,
an imprint of Tundra Book Group, a division of Penguin Random House of Canada Limited

LIBRARY OF CONGRESS CONTROL NUMBER: 2021943763

Edited by Tara Walker with assistance from Margot Blankier
Designed by John Martz
The artwork in this book was drawn with watercolor, pencil, a pinch of Photoshop and gallons of coffee.
The text was set in Historical Fell Type Roman.

I am very grateful for the help of Peggy Perdue, Toronto-based Doylean and rare books librarian, who reviewed this book and shared invaluable knowledge and experience in her feedback. Any errors, omissions or inaccuracies are my own.

Huge thanks go to Tara Walker for her editorial excellence and encouragement, to Margot Blankier for her Sherlock-sharp eye and TLC, and to the great Tundra team of John Martz, Katelyn Chan and Kate Doyle. Special thanks to Isabelle Follath for her delightful marriage of Victorian accuracy and tongue-in-cheek humor in the art.

— Linda Bailey

PRINTED IN CHINA

www.penguinrandomhouse.ca

1 2 3 4 5   26 25 24 23 22

tundra | Penguin Random House
TUNDRA BOOKS

ARTHUR WHO WROTE SHERLOCK

WRITTEN BY
Linda Bailey

ILLUSTRATED BY
Isabelle Follath

tundra

What if you wrote a story about a detective,
and he became the most famous detective ever?
What if the whole *world* loved your detective?
Wouldn't that be wonderful?

Or . . . would it?

From the very beginning, Arthur loves stories.

Here he is with his mother and sister. As his mother stirs the porridge, she tells a thrilling story of knights of long ago. Brave heroes! Terrible foes! In the spooky parts, her voice sinks to a whisper . . .

"MORE!" says Arthur.

When Arthur is still very young, his mother teaches him to read. Soon he's a regular visitor at the library. He goes there so often, the library makes a new rule — only two book exchanges a day!

When Arthur is six, he writes his first story. It's about a man who gets into a fight with a Bengal tiger. (Guess who wins?) Arthur learns his first lesson about writing. "It is very easy to get people *into* scrapes," he says, "and very hard to get them *out* again."

Arthur is lucky to have stories. They help him through the tough parts of his life.

One tough part is money. His family doesn't have enough. They have to keep moving, looking for cheaper places to rent in their home city, Edinburgh. And when Arthur outgrows his clothes, there's not always money for new ones. It's not fair.

It's also not fair that Arthur's father is mentally ill. He has
problems with alcohol, and when he can't work, there is even less
money. Sometimes he steals from his children's coin boxes.

When Arthur is nine, he is sent away to boarding school. (His uncles, who are wealthy, pay his fees.)

It's not fair that Arthur can go home only six weeks a year. It's not fair that when he gets in trouble, he gets whacked on the hands — HARD! — with a big rubber whacker. The food is awful, and the classes are boring. Arthur's report cards say that he is noisy, sulky, messy, lazy and scatterbrained.

But he loves sports — and fortunately, he still has stories! Here is Arthur a few years later with a group of younger boys. Like his mother, he's an excellent storyteller. He knows when to shout and when to whisper. He knows the *exact right moment* to stop —

"MORE!" yell the boys.

"Does anyone have anything to eat?" asks Arthur. Some boys have treats: an apple, a tart, a bit of cake. They rush to hand them over.

"Thank you," says Arthur, and he finishes the story.

When Arthur is seventeen, he goes to medical school. While he is there, he gets a lucky break. He is chosen to be the assistant of his favorite teacher, Dr. Joseph Bell.

Dr. Bell is a whiz! He can figure out all kinds of things about a patient without asking a single question. Job? Home? Family? Dr. Bell can guess them in an instant.

It looks like magic — but it's simple. Dr. Bell *observes*. He watches people like a hawk. (He even looks like a hawk!) He notices tiny, telltale clues.

Arthur is amazed.

At medical school, Arthur is still poor. He has only two pennies for lunch each day — enough for a meat pie. But on the way to the pies, there's a bookstore. It has a barrel of books out front with a sign that says, "Your choice for two pennies!"

Most days, Arthur eats a pie for lunch. But he can't help peeking in the barrel. And once or twice a week, he buys a *book* instead . . .

And goes hungry.

Because Arthur is poor, he has to take breaks from his studies to earn money. And because he loves adventure, he goes to sea. He takes a job as a medical officer on a whaling ship. Arthur loves the frozen North. He gets so excited about the ice floes that he falls into the Arctic Ocean — five times in four days!

His next job is on a
steamship going to Africa.
Again, the trip is exciting.
First his ship hits
a huge storm!

Then he gets a terrible fever!

Then he goes for a
swim and is *almost*
eaten by a shark!

Then his ship catches fire!
(Arthur doesn't know it, but
soon these adventures will come
in handy.)

When Arthur becomes a doctor, he is still poor. He rents an office and buys used furniture for it, but he can't afford to furnish the back room where he lives.

Does this bother Arthur? Not a bit! A gas lamp on the wall is his stove. A travel trunk is both cupboard and table. And a stool makes a fine chair.

Every day, he waits for patients to come. And waits. And waits.

The good part is — Arthur has time to write stories!

He tries all kinds. Thinking about his own life, he makes up stories about sea travel and medicine. He also writes about history and ghosts and exotic adventures. (He likes history the best!) He rolls his stories into mailing tubes and sends them to publishers, hoping they'll be published.

Most of the tubes get sent right back. Rejected! Arthur jokes that his stories are just going on a holiday. He calls it "the circular tour."

One day, he tries writing a detective story. He needs a detective, of course. But what kind?

And then he remembers his old teacher — Dr. Bell. Yes, by Jove, that's IT! Arthur's detective will be brilliant and scientific. He will *observe* things. He will examine clues like a hawk and see things that ordinary people miss. He will even *look* like a hawk.

His name will be Sherrington Hope. No, wait — Sherrinford Holmes! No, wait —

Sherlock Holmes

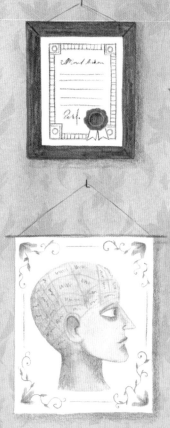

Arthur writes a novella (a long story) about Sherlock called
A Study in Scarlet. Three publishers say no. BOO! But when it's
finally published, readers like it. HOORAY! But then they soon
forget it. BOO!

Arthur keeps writing. Months go by. Years. Slowly, more stories
get published, including another novella called *The Sign of the Four*.
Slowly, more patients come to Arthur's office. For a while, he tries to
become an eye doctor.

Then one day, he has an idea. What if he wrote *a series of short
mystery stories* about his genius detective — to be published regularly
in the same magazine? Readers could have new Sherlock stories all
the time! Will they get excited, waiting for the next story?

The answer is . . . YES! For the next year, *The Strand Magazine* publishes a brand-new Sherlock story every month. People ADORE them! The more they get to know this quirky, brilliant — and sometimes hilarious — detective, the better they like him. They also like his not-quite-so-clever partner, Dr. Watson. Soon people are lining up to buy copies!

They're fascinated by the strange crimes.

They're gripped by the clever writing.

And they can't *wait* to see how the mysteries will be solved.

Sherlock is a SENSATION!

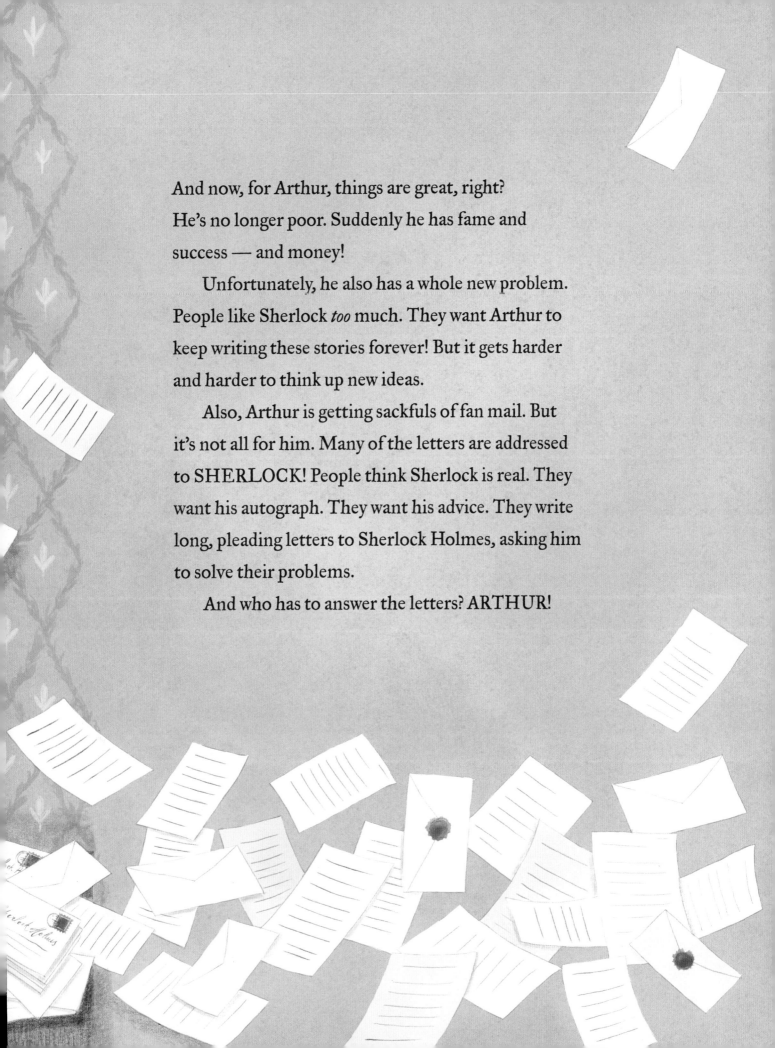

And now, for Arthur, things are great, right? He's no longer poor. Suddenly he has fame and success — and money!

Unfortunately, he also has a whole new problem. People like Sherlock *too* much. They want Arthur to keep writing these stories forever! But it gets harder and harder to think up new ideas.

Also, Arthur is getting sackfuls of fan mail. But it's not all for him. Many of the letters are addressed to SHERLOCK! People think Sherlock is real. They want his autograph. They want his advice. They write long, pleading letters to Sherlock Holmes, asking him to solve their problems.

And who has to answer the letters? ARTHUR!

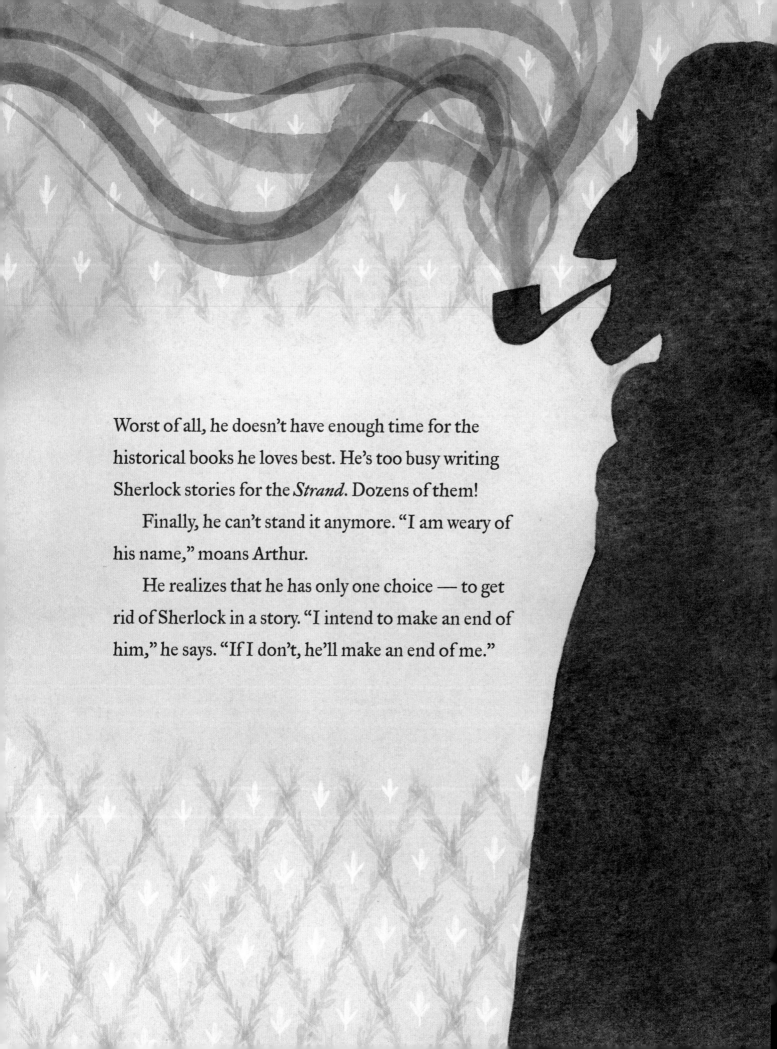

Worst of all, he doesn't have enough time for the historical books he loves best. He's too busy writing Sherlock stories for the *Strand*. Dozens of them!

Finally, he can't stand it anymore. "I am weary of his name," moans Arthur.

He realizes that he has only one choice — to get rid of Sherlock in a story. "I intend to make an end of him," he says. "If I don't, he'll make an end of me."

On a trip to Switzerland, Arthur visits a famous waterfall.
It's dizzyingly high, and it plunges into a roaring abyss.
If a person were to fall over the Reichenbach Falls . . .
he would *never* survive.

Arthur writes "The Final Problem."
In this story, Sherlock faces an enemy as brilliant
as *he* is — the evil genius Moriarty. Moriarty
must be stopped! Sherlock gives it his all! But
in the end, he and Moriarty are locked in a
deadly wrestling match. Where? At the top
of the Reichenbach Falls! No one is there
to see when the two men slip . . .
And plunge over the falls
to their deaths!

"Killed Holmes,"
writes Arthur in his diary.

Whew! Arthur feels much better. His problem is solved, right?
But then people read the new story...

WHAT??? SHERLOCK *DEAD*???

The world goes into a frenzy! Newspapers announce Sherlock's death — as if he were real! People *weep* when they hear.

Twenty thousand readers immediately cancel their subscriptions to the *Strand*. Angry letters from Sherlock fans pour in to Arthur. One begins with the words "You brute!" Poor Arthur! Is it true that a strange woman has walked up to him in the street and whacked him with her purse? Even the royal family is upset!

People *beg* Arthur to change his mind. No, he says.
And for the next eight years, he writes what he wants.
(Not Sherlock!)

Then he gets a new idea — about a dog. But not
just any dog. This dog is a legend! A gigantic, terrifying
GHOST HOUND that wanders the lonely
English moors at night. Arthur *loves* this idea. But it
needs . . . a detective.

YES! Arthur is finally ready to write another Sherlock
Holmes story. It's called *The Hound of the Baskervilles*.
This story is so good, and readers like it so much, and Arthur
is offered so much money — that he keeps on going.
MORE Sherlock stories!

But wait! How can this be? Sherlock is *dead*!

Arthur comes up with an explanation. That fight at the top of Reichenbach Falls? Sherlock didn't *really* plunge to the bottom and die. Instead he used a special kind of wrestling called "baritsu" to slip free — and escape! He's been *hiding ever since in Tibet and other faraway lands* to throw off Moriarty's gang.

Fig. 1

Fig. 2

Fig. 3

Do you believe this explanation? Arthur's readers do. They're so happy to have Sherlock back, they'd believe anything!

And so, Sherlock Holmes goes on solving mysteries — dozens more. Everyone is happy. Even Arthur! He now writes Sherlock stories only when he *chooses* to.

But what about the rest of Arthur's life? It is long and very active. He marries twice, has five children, travels the world, runs for government and plays all kinds of sports, including cricket, football, billiards, golf, boxing, bowling, skiing, cycling and . . . well, there's too much to tell, really.

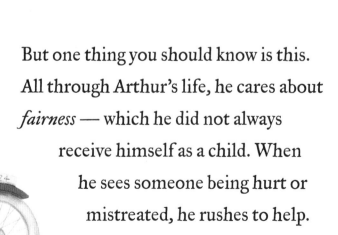

But one thing you should know is this. All through Arthur's life, he cares about *fairness* — which he did not always receive himself as a child. When he sees someone being hurt or mistreated, he rushes to help.

When he hears about people wrongly put in jail, he works tirelessly to free them. He even assists the police, now and then, to solve real-life crimes.

But mostly Arthur's sense of justice comes out — where? Why, in Sherlock, of course! A detective so brilliant, he can always discover the truth and make things right.

"GEORGE EDALJI IS INNOCENT" SAYS SIR ARTHUR CONAN DOYLE.

Arthur died a long time ago — in 1930. Many of his books are now mostly forgotten.

But Sherlock? *Sherlock has become a legend!* He goes on and on, and his adventures are more popular than ever. Books, movies, television, plays — Sherlock is everywhere. He's been called "the world's most famous man who never was!"

And if you are like most people in the world, you will know his name. Sherlock Holmes.

But what about Arthur? The writer who made up every word? Do you know *his* name? Here it is now, in big bold letters so you will always remember . . .

ARTHUR CONAN DOYLE

Thanks, Arthur!

AUTHOR'S NOTE

For years, I had been curious about Arthur Conan Doyle (born 1859, died 1930). I knew the story — how he had killed off his famous detective — and in fact, I had often told it in school visits that focused on the mystery genre. But it took me a surprisingly long time to pick up some Conan Doyle biographies in the library.

I was stopped, I think, by the online photos. Staring at the black-and-white images of this walrus-mustached Victorian gentleman in his stiff suits, I remember thinking . . . stuffy. Staid. Stodgy.

I was wrong, of course. I learned very quickly that, far from being stuffy, Arthur's life was filled with both fascinating adventures and comical misadventures. Where to start? He got kicked in the head by a horse he was riding in Egypt — and later wrote an ingenious story in which a "murder" victim dies by horse-kick. (Yes, that's right. The *horse* did it!) He attended séances with a skeptical Harry Houdini. He once "skied" down a Swiss mountain slope on his own tweedy backside because, as an early pioneer of the sport, he accidentally sent his skis down first.

The more I read, the more the phrase "larger-than-life" came to mind. And in fact, Arthur was *literally* large. A tall, burly man, he was once described by a reporter as looking "like two policemen rolled into one." But more to the point, he *lived* large — fully, energetically and with enormous gusto. This made him a likeable research subject . . . but a hard guy to sandwich into a picture book!

His tale began with a heroically caring mother — a woman in tough circumstances who put her heart into giving her son a strong foundation. She encouraged him to read at a young age, and her storytelling was inspirational. Story, in fact, became one of Arthur's greatest gifts. In his early Sherlock years, after giving up his medical practice, he wrote at a blistering pace, creating fresh, imaginative and quickly beloved new stories month after month after month. But that same remarkable talent was also his downfall. In his own words, "The difficulty of the Holmes work was that every story really needed as clear-cut and original a plot as a longish book would do. One cannot without effort spin plots at such a rate." Eventually the strain became overwhelming.

At that point, Arthur felt he had only one choice — to "kill off" his main character. A simple solution, he thought. Unfortunately, he had done his job as a storyteller too well. He had created a character for the ages — and Sherlock's readers proved astonishingly unwilling to let him go.

Arthur, however, stayed firm in his choice and was not particularly troubled by the public outrage. Leaving Sherlock at the bottom of the Reichenbach Falls for a full eight years, he moved on to write "better things," as he put it. It wasn't until a compelling new story idea came along — one that happened to require a detective — that he considered a revival. By that point, he'd had a good long rest from Sherlock. He could set his own terms for a writing schedule. And after eight years, perhaps he also had an eye on his finances.

Arthur went on writing, including Sherlock stories, almost to the end of his life at age 71. But writing was far from his only interest. He was also a keen amateur athlete — a man who apparently never met a sport he didn't like. He was a husband and father in two successive families, his second marriage following the death of his first wife by tuberculosis. He was, twice and unsuccessfully, an aspiring politician running for Parliament. During the Boer War, he volunteered as a doctor and was later knighted by the king. And late in his life, he became an ardent spiritualist who gave lectures about communicating with the spirits of the dead. (This did not help his literary reputation, especially as he had created such a model of rationality in Sherlock Holmes.) He was also at times a passionate crusader on behalf of prisoners unjustly convicted of crimes. Most famously, he investigated and fought to overturn the wrongful conviction of George Edalji, a young Anglo-Indian lawyer victimized because of his race.

But it is Arthur's *written* work that lives on. In size alone, it is stunning. The Sherlock Holmes canon (4 novels and 56 short stories) was only a small part of his output. Altogether, he wrote 24 novels and more than 200 short stories, in addition to poems, plays and works of nonfiction. Sci-fi, adventure, humor, history, sports, military, medical, supernatural, crime — Arthur was comfortable in all these genres and often a pioneer.

His great and lasting legacy, of course, was the Sherlock stories. Key to their success was their wide appeal. They were gobbled up by all ages and classes at a time when pleasure reading was just beginning to be popularized in England. And because they were witty and gripping, with a fascinating detective and an endearingly loyal assistant in Dr. Watson, as well as striking illustrations by Sidney Paget, their appeal just grew and grew. Over the years, they have attracted millions of readers around the globe.

And now, more than a century later, Sherlock continues to flourish. He's the focus of hundreds of clubs and societies worldwide and features regularly in new movies, books and television series. In London, visitors still flock to his "home" at 221B Baker Street — or as close as they can get to that Arthur-invented address. Even the name "Sherlock" has been elevated to become a synonym for "detective." The character has become iconic.

And what would Arthur think of all this? Ultimately, he did grow fond of his hero. In a farewell he wrote to his readers in later years, he imagined "some fantastic limbo for the children of imagination," a kind of "Valhalla" where beloved fictional characters could meet and mingle at the end of their lives. Arthur hoped that in some humble corner, "Sherlock and his Watson may for a time find a place."

It's a wonderful image. I love to think that such a literary Valhalla does exist. And if so, surely it *must* include Sherlock Holmes — a brilliantly written and deeply beloved character who simply refuses to die.

Well done, Arthur.

SOURCES

Barnes, Julian. *Arthur & George*. Vintage Canada, 2006.

Booth, Martin. *The Doctor and the Detective: A Biography of Sir Arthur Conan Doyle*. Minotaur Books, 2000.

Boström, Mattias. *From Holmes to Sherlock: The Story of the Men and Women Who Created an Icon*. The Mysterious Press, 2017. First published 2013 by Piratförlaget.

Carr, John Dickson. *The Life of Sir Arthur Conan Doyle*. Harper & Brothers, 1949.

Dirda, Michael. *On Conan Doyle: Or, The Whole Art of Storytelling*. Princeton University Press, 2012.

Doyle, Arthur Conan. *The Complete Stories of Sherlock Holmes*. Wordsworth Editions Limited, 2007.

Doyle, Arthur Conan. *Memories & Adventures*. Oxford University Press, 1989. First published 1924 by Hodder and Stoughton.

Haining, Peter, ed. *A Sherlock Holmes Compendium*. Castle Books, 1980.

Lellenberg, Jon, Daniel Stashower, and Charles Foley. *Arthur Conan Doyle: A Life in Letters*. Penguin Press, 2007.

Lycett, Andrew. *Conan Doyle: The Man Who Created Sherlock Holmes*. Weidenfeld & Nicolson, 2007.

Miller, Russell. *The Adventures of Arthur Conan Doyle*. Thomas Dunne Books, 2008.

Montague, Charlotte. *Creating Sherlock Holmes: The Remarkable Story of Sir Arthur Conan Doyle*. Chartwell Books, 2017.

Pugh, Brian W. *A Chronology of the Life of Sir Arthur Conan Doyle*. Andrews UK Limited, 2018.

Sims, Michael. *Arthur and Sherlock: Conan Doyle and the Creation of Holmes*. Bloomsbury Publishing, 2017.

ONLINE

Barquin, Alexis, ed. *The Arthur Conan Doyle Encyclopedia*, https://www.arthur-conan-doyle.com.

The description of Sherlock as "the world's most famous man who never was" has been attributed to Orson Welles.